Guess the Baby

Simon French
and
Donna Rawlins

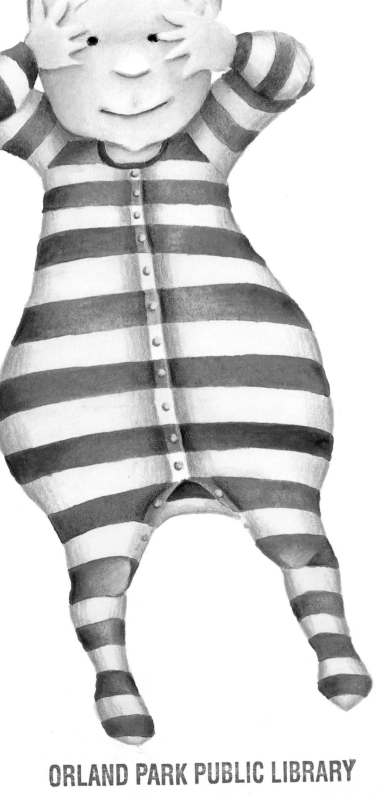

Clarion Books
New York

For Tiarna, Jordan, Maddi and Morgan—
and all my Kindergarten pupils,
past and present.
SF

For Henry Callum, Ishbel, Alfie, Felix,
Olivia, Bridget, Morag, Finola,
Joe and Callum.
DR

Clarion Books
a Houghton Mifflin Company imprint
215 Park Avenue South, New York, NY 10003
Text copyright © 2002 by Simon French
Illustrations copyright © 2002 by Donna Rawlins

First published in Australia in 2002 by ABC Books for the Australian Broadcasting
Corporation, GPO Box 9994, Sydney, NSW 2001. First published in the United States in 2002.

The illustrations were executed in acrylic gouache and colored pencils.
The text was set in 18-point Stone Informal.

www.houghtonmifflinbooks.com

Printed in Singapore.

Library of Congress Cataloging-in-Publication Data

French, Simon, 1957–
Guess the baby / by Simon French ; illustrated by Donna Rawlins.
p. cm.
Summary: When Sam brings his baby brother to school for Show and Tell, it provides
Mr. Judd with an opportunity to teach the class some things about babies,
including that even grown-ups were babies once.
ISBN 0-618-25989-9
[1. Babies—Fiction. 2. Schools—Fiction.] I. Rawlins, Donna, ill. II.Title.
PZ7.F8875 Gu 2002
[Fic]—dc21   2002002747

10 9 8 7 6 5 4 3 2 1

When Sam's baby brother came to school for
Show and Tell, Sam told us, "He's called Jake. He
has a green carriage, he eats mushy baby food . . .

. . . and sometimes his diapers are really yucky."
Everyone laughed, even Sam's mom and our
teacher, Mr. Judd.

"But that's okay," Mr. Judd said. "After all, Jake is a baby. And everyone was a baby once."

I thought Sam's baby brother looked as tiny as a doll. His face was little. His arms and legs were little. His toes were little. Everything was little.

We watched baby Jake being bathed and fed. We took turns talking to him, and we talked together about the things it took to look after a baby.

"They need special foods," said Mara.

"They need to be picked up and hugged," said Jack.

"They cry," said Chi.

"And sometimes they smell," said Tess.

Mr. Judd asked us to bring our baby photos to school, to show how much we'd grown and changed. He put them on the bulletin board. "But you can't say which baby is you," he told us. "We have to try to guess."

So we did. All the babies looked kind of alike at first.

A lot of them had no teeth to smile with,
and some of them had no hair.

But we guessed Jack, because of his curly hair. And
Anika, because her eyes were so big and dark. We
guessed Sacha, because he still has the same smile.

And Mara, because
her hair is as orange
as oranges.

We guessed Ben and Kyle and Greta and Tess.

We guessed Naomi and Chi and Sam and Braydon.

And Hannah guessed me. "I thought it was you," she said. "I don't know why. I just *knew*."

Mr. Judd helped us with the tricky ones. "This baby is a girl, and now she's very fast at doing puzzles," he said. And, "This is a boy, and now he's a terrific dancer."

"It's Jade!" we guessed. "It's Ryan!"

But the last baby was the hardest of all. We thought
we had guessed everyone in the room. Who was this?

Mr. Judd smiled a wide smile. He said,
"This baby grew up to be *very* handsome.
And very clever. But even though this baby
is very grown up, he's still at school."

"Mr. Judd!" we all shouted. "It's Mr. Judd
when he was a baby!"

"Mr. Judd didn't know how to write his name," said Mara.

"Mr. Judd used to eat mushy baby food," said Tess.

"Mr. Judd used to have yucky diapers," said Kyle.

"Mr. Judd used to ride in a baby carriage because
he was too little to drive a car," said Jack.

Mr. Judd laughed. "See?" he said. "I used to be as little
as Sam's brother. Even grownups were babies once."

And I said, "One day, babies and kids get to be grownups."

"But not for a long time yet," said Mr. Judd. "Hands
up if you like being a kid! A big kid at school."